Lucy Buckley - the author. Born 12.08.1999.

Lucy loves dancing, swimming, running and karate. Lucy has supported her brother James with Look For Loneliness and has helped him immensely by writing this wonderful story. She is caring, loving and always always Looks For Loneliness.

Chloe's Big Change

Lucy is ten years old. She is the nicest little girl you could meet. She is kind, loving and giving. She wants to be everybody's friend and hates to see anyone cry. But because Lucy is a pretty girl who makes friends very easily, sometimes other girls are jealous of her.

It was an ordinary Monday morning, however, Lucy woke very early. She was very excited. Her teacher had told her class that there was a new girl starting today.

When Lucy arrived at school, she went to hang up her coat. She could hear a nasty little girl called Chloe telling some other girls not to speak to the new girl because she was weird. Lucy felt very sad that Chloe was being nasty again.

"Chloe, you really should try to get to know the new girl before you say nasty things about her," Lucy said.

"Oh shut up goody two shoes," Chloe said nastily as she pushed past Lucy, her gang following her.

Lucy went to her class a little shaken. She spotted the new girl straight away. Lucy went to her and asked, "Are you OK? You're new to the school aren't you?"

"Yyyes I am new. My name is Layla," she said nervously.

Layla had a bad stutter and this meant that some words she found very difficult to say. Being nervous didn't help and today her stutter was worse than ever.

Mrs. Hudson had seated Layla and Lucy together. Lucy felt very proud to be looking after Layla. She helped her find her way around the school. She showed her which books to use. At playtime they stayed together. Layla didn't speak much. Lucy wasn't bothered, she found games to play with Layla and really liked the new girl. Soon the other girls and boys began to play with Layla too.

Lucy and Layla had lunch together. Layla spoke a little but only when she knew no one could hear her. The lunch room cleared and Lucy and Layla were left alone together. Little did they know that Chloe was listening near by.

"I hhhate starting new schools," Layla said. "My dad mmmmoves jobs a lot. IIIII have b b been to four d d d d different schools already."

"Well I hope you will be here a long time. I think you are a nice friend." Lucy always found something nice to say.

"Thank you. I know that w w when the others hear me speak they'll be c c c cruel. I I it always h h h appens."

"Don't worry," Lucy put her arm around Layla. "I like you."

The children went to their lessons. Layla and Lucy were split up for the afternoon. Lucy went to Art and Layla went to Computer Studies.

At afternoon playtime Lucy went to find Layla. Layla was sitting on a bench, crying.

Lucy ran to her, "Layla what's happened?" When Layla saw Lucy she began shouting and throwing her arms about in the air. Lucy couldn't understand what Layla was saying. She was obviously very upset. What could be the matter?

"What is wrong Layla? Why are you upset?" Lucy asked calmly.

Layla took a deep breath.
"You know what the m m m matter is! I know the n n nasty things you've been saying about m m me. Y y you said you liked me," Layla sobbed. "It's the same wherever I go."

Lucy felt terrible. She hadn't said anything bad about Layla. She wanted to be her friend and help her. Lucy really didn't know what to say.

As Lucy turned to go back into school she saw Chloe laughing with her gang of girls.

"Layla, Layla come here and play with us," Chloe shouted.

As Lucy walked past Chloe and her friends, they said awful things.

"Some friend you are…."
"You're a mean girl…"
"What's Layla ever done to you…."

Lucy ran to her classroom and began to cry. The rest of the class soon came inside. The other children carried on saying horrible things to Lucy.
"Layla, please believe me I haven't said anything about you," Lucy said firmly.

"Chloe t t ttold me you were doing impressions o o o of me. H h h how I I I speak. I know it's you, I haven't spoken to anyone else."

Lucy couldn't get a word in. She couldn't explain what had happened. She felt so sad.

As Layla left school that day, she overheard Chloe laughing and telling another trouble maker what trouble she'd caused for Lucy.

"I heard Layla talking to Lucy after lunch and she can't speak properly. I've told everyone that Lucy was being nasty about Layla. Ha ha serves Miss Goody Two Shoes right. I hate her. She hasn't any friends now."

Layla was horrified. She froze to the spot. Suddenly she felt so angry. Chloe had made her first day at her new school horrible.

Layla's mummy was waiting for her outside school. She walked straight past her mummy, straight up to Chloe who was standing with her daddy. Layla hated speaking in front of people. Her heart was beating so loudly and her mouth was dry but, she was so very angry.

"Chloe," Layla began, "I know what you did today - I heard you telling Jack. You are a bully, you are unkind, selfish and jealous of Lucy."

Chloe's face turned red. What could she say?

"I've been bullied before and I know a lot about bullying," Layla continued. "You are not going to bully me whilst I am at this school."

"Chloe's not a bully," Sarah, one of Chloe's friends said. "She hasn't hit you."

"You don't have to hit anyone to be a bully. Chloe is a bully. She has made lies up about Lucy and turned everyone against her. She has enjoyed embarrassing me and hurting Lucy. Sarah, you go along with Chloe to save yourself being bullied. You all need to be taught a big lesson." Layla finished and walked back to her mum.

"Layla I am so proud of you. You said that so well," her mum said.

All Layla had to do now was put things right with Lucy. But how?

Layla asked her mum to take her to school early the next day. She needed to speak to Lucy before lessons started.

As Layla entered her classroom she was shocked to see Chloe sitting at her desk looking very upset.

"I am so sorry Layla. I went home last night feeling very very bad. I couldn't get to sleep. I want to change but I don't know how," Chloe started to cry.

Layla knew it would be hard for Chloe to stop bullying and change her ways. Layla knew she could help her especially with Lucy's assistance.

"I c c ccan help you to stop b b being a bully. But it will take t t ttime. First thing you must do is explain to Lucy what you did y yyesterday."

Lucy came to school looking very pale and upset. She didn't look at anyone as she entered her classroom.

Layla touched her arm as she sat down.
"Lucy, I know y y yyou didn't say those awful things about me y y yyesterday. I'm sorry I accused you and hope w wwe can be friends again," Layla stuttered.

Lucy smiled from ear to ear. "Of course we can. But what...?"

"I heard Layla talking to you after lunch yesterday. You looked really happy - perfect friends. It made me feel angry, I wanted to make you both unhappy, so I made up lies about you Lucy," Chloe blurted out. "I don't like what I did, I'm sorry and embarrassed."
Lucy looked at her in disbelief. She was so shocked.

"Right, lesson one," Layla announced. "You n n n need to think of one good thing about everyone in this class. Whenever you feel like you w w wwant to upset someone, you need to think of the g g g good thought. It will t t ttake a while, but soon you will make r r real friends and earn respect. You don't want your friends to fear you," Layla lectured.

Over the next few weeks, Layla taught Chloe many lessons. Layla had been bullied for as long as she could remember. When Layla left her last school she had spent time learning about why people bully. Layla knew it was hard to stop being a bully but she enjoyed helping Chloe. Lucy enjoyed watching Layla's confidence grow as she helped Chloe change her ways.

Layla knew that bullies usually lacked confidence themselves and that they felt better about themselves when they made others feel worse. Chloe's main task was to ask adults to tell her the things they found good about her. Chloe found out lots of good things when she asked around.

Lucy, Layla and Chloe soon became the best of friends. They trusted each other and told each other many secrets. Chloe loved having true friends. How different she felt.

Remember.......Bullying is only successful if you don't do anything about it.

Always..........

Look For Loneliness

Published by
Look For Loneliness

Author
Lucy J Buckley

If you are a child or young person needing help you can call
ChildLine on 0800 1111.
ChildLine is the UK's free, confidential 24-hour helpline for children and young people.
If you're deaf, hard of hearing or speech impaired,
You can text phone 0800 400 222.